T0413306

PUMA

BY MARIE JASKULKA

Content Consultant
Kelly A. Cobb, MFA
Associate Professor of Fashion
and Apparel Studies
University of Delaware

Essential Library

An Imprint of Abdo Publishing
abdobooks.com

ABDOBOOKS.COM

THIS BOOK CONTAINS RECYCLED MATERIALS

Cover Photo: Kin Cheung/AP Images
Interior Photos: Shutterstock Images, 4–5, 6, 20, 34–35, 55, 56–57, 76–77, 84, 87; Vitaliy Andreev/Shutterstock Images, 12; Karl Schnoerrer/Picture Alliance/Getty Images, 14–15; Christof Stache/AP Images, 22–23; Kurt Rohwedder/Picture Alliance/Getty Images, 28–29; Keystone-France/Gamma-Rapho/Getty Images, 33; AP Images, 36, 42, 48–49; Angelo Cozzi/Mario De Biasi/Sergio Del Grande/Mondadori Portfolio/Getty Images, 39; Robert Dear/AP Images, 44; Al Bello/Hulton Archive/Getty Images, 52; Frank Mächler/Picture Alliance/Getty Images, 59; Rick Friedman/Corbis Historical/Getty Images, 61; Gail Oskin/Wire Image for Puma/Getty Images, 64; Andy Kropa/Invision/AP Images, 66; Christof Stache/AFP/Getty Images, 68–69, 72, 80–81; Ulrich Baumgarten/Getty Images, 74; Nattawit Khomsanit/Shutterstock Images, 86; Qiongna Liao/Shutterstock Images, 88–89; Jean Catuffe/Getty Images Sport/Getty Images, 93; Simon Dawson/Bloomberg/Getty Images, 95; Moses Robinson/Getty Images for PUMA/Getty Images Entertainment/Getty Images, 99

Editor: Arnold Ringstad
Series Designer: Sarah Taplin

Library of Congress Control Number: 2021951560
Publisher's Cataloging-in-Publication Data
Names: Jaskulka, Marie, author.
Title: Puma / by Marie Jaskulka.
Description: Minneapolis, Minnesota : Abdo Publishing, 2023 | Series: Sports brands | Includes online resources and index.
Identifiers: ISBN 9781532198151 (lib. bdg.) | ISBN 9781098271800 (ebook)
Subjects: LCSH: Clothing and dress--Juvenile literature. | PUMA AG Rudolf Dassler Sport--Juvenile literature. | Sport clothes industry--Juvenile literature. | Brand name products--Juvenile literature.
Classification: DDC 338.7--dc23

CONTENTS

CHAPTER ONE

FOREVER FASTER

J ane spotted the giant jumping cat logo from a block away, and she knew they were close. In Jane's mind, the highlight of her family's trip to New York City was Puma NYC, the flagship store on Fifth Avenue where she planned to try on all the Calis that just dropped and stop by one of the in-store style events. Then she'd browse two floors of the most innovative athletic gear on the planet and try out the immersive experiences.

Jane stepped through the doors and immediately snapped selfies in front of a Puma NYC sign and a giant photo of soccer player Nikita Parris. Jane's absolute favorite cleats were the Puma Ones she bought after she saw Parris wear them in the FA Cup,

> *Puma's Fifth Avenue flagship store in New York City showcases the best the brand has to offer.*

a tournament in her native England. Jane loved how they grabbed the soccer field when she played. And the evoKNIT material made the shoes feel custom-made for her feet. Her friends didn't believe the shoes could have such a big effect, but she swore the footwear improved her game.

Scanning the store, Jane tried to see everything at once: the merch, the sneakers, the tech experiences, and most of all, the people. Pro athletes sometimes visited Puma NYC, especially Puma ambassadors. Scrolling through the store's Instagram feed, Jane often dreamed about attending the events in the posts. Olympians, soccer superstars, and basketball players were just some of the people who stopped by.

Before Jane could even reach the shoes, her brother began to beg their father to let them try the Formula 1 (F1) racing simulators, one of the store's immersive experiences. Jane's dad purchased tickets. Jane and her brother held their tickets up to a screen that said, "Scan your race ticket here." Next, they each jumped onto their own F1 racing simulators. According to a clerk, they were the same simulators professional F1 racers like Lewis Hamilton used to practice. The simulators rumbled and roared, making Jane feel as if she were really racing through the streets of New York City that were projected on a big screen in front of them.

When Jane finally got to the shoes, she walked right past the Calis to check out all the cleats she'd never seen in the stores back home. She tried on a pair of Ultra 1.3s, switched through a few different colors in the interactive mirrors, and then

RACE TO PUMA NYC

Professional F1 racing simulators allow visitors to the Puma NYC flagship store to experience a day at work for star racers like Lewis Hamilton and Max Verstappen. A giant screen in front of the vehicles displays the driver's point of view during a race through New York City that ends with a sprint down Forty-Ninth Street to a virtual image of the store's entrance. Hamilton and Verstappen deliver encouragement to riders through a surround sound system.

tested them out in the Skill Cube, a simulator where she experienced walking across the field of a world-famous arena. Jane begged to spend more time in the Skill Cube, so her dad took her brother to the basketball section of the store so he could play the latest version of *NBA 2K*.

They all wanted to customize their own Pumas in the Puma x You studio. Jane loved both soccer and fashion. That's part of why she liked Puma so much. Puma seemed to be made for peak performance and standout style. The company always seemed to be collaborating with the same designers Jane saw in fashion, such as Maison Kitsuné and Alexander-John. Plus, Puma always featured the coolest people in their ads. Pumas seemed to be created by fashion designers instead of mere shoemakers. By the time Jane's family checked out, they all loved Puma as

MAGIC MIRRORS

One high-tech feature of the Puma NYC flagship store is the interactive magic mirrors. Just like any retail shoe store, customers can try on a pair of Pumas. But the mirrors take this process to a new level. The mirrors allow users to snap digital photos from various angles and try on clothes and shoes virtually. Throughout the flagship store, the magic mirrors help customers envision how shoes and apparel might fit and look in different sizes or colors. The mirrors provide links to online commerce sites to help customers find an ideal product.

much as Jane did. She put on her Puma NYC hoodie and posted a selfie with the hashtag #futurePumaAthlete.

THE DASSLER BROTHERS' SECRET TO SELLING SNEAKERS

Early in the 1900s, two brothers named Adolf (Adi) and Rudolf (Rudi) Dassler opened a shoe factory in their parents' laundry room in a small town in Germany. One brother made great shoes. The other had an extraordinary talent for selling them. Together, they sold a lot of athletic shoes by having whole teams wear them. When athletes wore the shoes during game-changing moments,

Retail consultants at Green Room Design developed the Puma NYC flagship store's Skill Cube. Inside this square room, visitors can test out their Puma gear on a hyperrealistic simulation of the field in Italy's historic San Siro Stadium. The walls of the Skill Cube display a highly realistic wraparound immersive video that transports users to a virtual stadium filled with 80,000 cheering soccer fans and five million individually rendered blades of grass.[1] In the Skill Cube, visitors can practice their skills with virtual coaching from some of the most famous faces in professional soccer, such as Romelu Lukaku and Antoine Griezmann.

newspapers ran photographs of the players. Often readers could see the shoes, bringing attention to the company. This was great free advertising.

In Europe at the time, the most popular team sport was soccer. The Dassler brothers started outfitting local soccer teams with shoes. Having famous athletes wear their brand in public ended up being a very good idea for the brothers. Adi and Rudi Dassler grew a thriving business together. Soon Olympic athletes were winning gold medals while wearing their shoes. It all seemed perfect until several rifts built up to an intense disagreement between the brothers. The controversial argument divided the Dassler family forever and drove the brothers apart.

COOL COLLABORATIONS

In 2021, Puma announced a collaboration with a design duo based in Milan, Italy, and Shanghai, China. Pronounce, made up of Yushan Li and Jun Zhou, would create a line of apparel, footwear, and accessories. The high-end brand Pronounce creates clothing that is both global and genderless, combining inspirations from cultures and philosophies all over the world. The Puma x Pronounce collection draws its inspiration from an archaeological site in Bolivia called Pumapunku that was home to the ancient Inca. The colors in the line—orange, pebble, and muted gray—are reminiscent of the sunset over the site.

THE EVER-EVOLVING PUMA

Both brothers set out to use what they had learned together to build even better shoe businesses on their own. From the start, Rudi Dassler and his company Puma didn't just manufacture shoes. He constantly improved the shoes' design by partnering with experts such as winning coaches, professional players, and amateurs who were on the road to stardom. He asked questions to better understand athletes' needs and limitations, including their specific complaints about play surfaces. Then he adjusted the designs. The resulting products were a constantly improving line of shoes that solved athletes' problems so they could perform better. The concept of going back to the drawing board and updating past designs based on new data is a recurring theme throughout Puma's 70-year history.

As Rudi grew Puma, his brother Adi built his own shoe business called Adidas. With the formation of these two companies, the Dassler brothers entered an era of fierce rivalry that would last the rest of their lives and beyond. Always innovating, the competitive brothers were motivated to outdo one another. They used athlete endorsements to build two of the world's most successful sports brands.

Today, Puma still maintains its ranking as one of the world's leading sports brands, and the Dassler brothers' rivalry still impacts the business. Puma partners with some of the most successful athletes on the planet to develop state-of-the-art products that improve athletic performance. Many professional teams proudly display

the Puma jumping cat logo on their team jerseys and shoes. Fans and players alike show their allegiance to the brand by buying Puma products and, just as importantly, avoiding Adidas.

Puma now partners with influencers and fashion icons as well as standout athletes. The results are shoes and apparel as trendy and fashionable as they are useful in sports. Puma has also made a promise through its #Reform program to support athletes who raise their voices to fight for justice and acceptance of all people, regardless of race, gender, or sexual orientation. This long-standing international innovator in the sportswear industry has a rich history and tradition, but fans of the brand believe Puma is just getting warmed up.

> *Puma's shoes have become famous for their mix of fashion and functionality.*

CHAPTER TWO

BROTHERS DIVIDED

I t seems almost inevitable that the Dassler brothers ended up in the shoe business. They grew up in Herzogenaurach, a small German town split by the Aurach River. Long before the Dassler brothers were born, the town became known as a center of shoemaking. Factories in Herzogenaurach created mass quantities of "Schlappen," or felt slippers. Christoph Dassler, Adi and Rudi's father, was a shoemaker, so his tools and knowledge were available to the brothers.

After serving in World War I (1914–1918), Adi returned to Herzogenaurach and began collecting scraps of fabric from old army gear. He used them to assemble work shoes in the laundry room of his

> *Rudi Dassler created Puma after a wartime split with his brother, Adi.*

Herzogenaurach, a small Bavarian town on the banks of the Aurach River, was already known for manufacturing and weaving when the Dassler brothers were young. In fact, the Dassler brothers' father worked in a shoe factory. When the brothers' business broke up, the rift affected the entire town for decades. At times, Puma and Adidas were the largest employers in Herzogenaurach, and the employees of one company wouldn't speak to employees of the other. The town has owed much of its economic prosperity to the two shoe companies and often incorporates the Puma and Adidas logos on town property such as manhole covers.

parents' home. Like many entrepreneurs, Adi started by making products for his friends. When word of the shoes' quality got around, Adi began to sell more, and his older brother Rudi joined his business. They named their business Gebrüder Dassler Schuhfabrik, or Geda for short. The full name translated to Dassler Brothers Shoe Factory. The founding mantra of their business was "Our strength lies in specialization."[1] *Specialization* referred to the thought the brothers put into building and improving their shoes, but it also summarized the brothers' approach of recognizing their strengths and dividing the work in the company. From the beginning, Adi focused on production, while Rudi specialized in sales. Adi quietly tinkered away producing shoes while Rudi excelled at getting in front of people and selling the shoes.

Geda achieved a major success at the 1936 Berlin Olympics. Athletes wearing Geda shoes earned seven gold medals and five bronze medals, but one Olympic athlete stood out from the others that year.[2] Rudi and Adi had campaigned hard to convince runner Jesse Owens to wear Geda shoes when he competed in the Olympics. Owens agreed, and he went on to win four gold medals, set a world record in the 200-meter dash, and help to set the world record in the 4x100-meter relay.[3]

The shoe company hit a severe rough patch during World War II (1939–1945). Tensions among family members were already rising when Rudi was drafted to fight while Adi was deemed essential to the family business and allowed to stay in Herzogenaurach and manage the factory. Germany, under the control of the Nazi Party, converted businesses like the Dasslers' into manufacturers of weapons. The family business began to produce antitank weapons. Rudi fought on the

JESSE OWENS

The 1936 Summer Olympics in Berlin played out against the backdrop of German dictator Adolf Hitler's brutal and racist regime. Hitler wanted the Olympics to be a display of the Aryan people's athletic superiority over other races. To help promote this idea, Hitler decorated the Olympic stadium with Nazi propaganda. Black athlete Jesse Owens, the son of a sharecropper and the grandson of slaves, competed for the United States and often faced discrimination that his white teammates did not. Owens became a powerful symbol when his wins contradicted Hitler's false ideas about the supremacy of the Aryan race.

front lines, served time as a prisoner of war for a year, and then returned to Herzogenaurach. The factory returned to making shoes, but the brothers' relationship never went back to how it had been before the war. Instead, the brothers entered a serious fight that lasted for the rest of their lives.

DASSLER FAMILY DRAMA

While the brothers never disclosed the exact cause of their dispute, one of the leading theories is that Adi profited by extending Rudi's time involved in the war. While some critics argue that it sounds too much like a conspiracy theory, Rudi was repeatedly pulled back into the war after numerous attempts to return home. There are even some rumors that Adi and his wife reported Rudi to American investigators for working for the Gestapo, also known as the German Secret State Police. While Rudi spent a year at a camp for prisoners of war, Adi earned profits selling the shoes made famous by Jesse Owens to American soldiers.

For years, people have speculated on the exact reason for the fight. Some believe Adi played a part in Rudi being drafted and imprisoned for a year so that he could have the family business all to himself. Others argue that a fight between the brothers' spouses caused the rift. The families of both Adi and Rudi, including their wives, children, siblings, and mother, all lived together under one roof, which likely didn't help matters. Although no one can pinpoint the exact cause of the brothers' rift, the impact was felt by their employees and the entire town of Herzogenaurach.

RUDA

After more than 20 successful years in business, the Dassler Brothers Shoe Factory shut its doors in 1948. Adi and Rudi split the assets and went their separate ways. Rudi moved his mother and family to a new home south of the Aurach River. A month after the split, Rudi launched a new shoe business. Its name, Ruda, consisted of the first two letters of his first and last names. A year later, Adi opened a shoe business north of the Aurach River and named it Adidas, using the first three letters of his first and last names.

The breakup of the Dassler Brothers Shoe Factory began a rivalry that spread far beyond the Dassler family. Residents of Herzogenaurach picked a side and stayed loyal in just about every aspect of life, from where to shop for groceries to which sports team to support to whom they should marry. "The split between the Dassler brothers was to Herzogenaurach what the building of the Berlin Wall was for the German capital," explained one local journalist.[4] After World War II, the German city of Berlin was split into West Berlin and East Berlin. The United

> *Herzogenaurach has long been closely linked with the shoemaking industry.*

States, the United Kingdom, and France controlled West Berlin. The Soviet Union controlled East Berlin. In 1961, to stop citizens of the communist east from fleeing to the west, the Soviet Union erected a concrete and barbed-wire wall in the city that made crossing the border almost impossible.

As the two businesses grew, residents became so divided that Herzogenaurach became known as "the town of bent necks" because citizens tended to look at each other's shoes before starting a conversation with a stranger to make sure they were on the same side.[5] Adding to the division, Herzogenaurach's two soccer clubs were sponsored by the Dasslers' companies. The rivalry endured so long and brought about such animosity that journalists referred to the fight and its impact on the sports apparel industry as the "sneaker wars."[6] Both brothers died within five years of each other in the 1970s.

CHAPTER THREE

BECOMING PUMA

O n October 1, 1948, Rudi changed the name of his company, officially founding Puma. Thinking that the name Ruda failed to evoke feelings of athleticism, Rudi brainstormed for a word that could carry an entire brand, and he landed on *Puma*. Longtime Puma employee Helmut Fischer recalled, "Rudolf's vision was that all of his products would embody the characteristics of a puma cat: speed, strength, suppleness, endurance, and agility—the same attributes that a successful athlete needs."[1]

One of the first ways Rudi set out to distinguish Puma from its competition was through its logo. Rudi toyed with several Puma logo designs, including a cat jumping through a letter

> *The Puma logo was modeled on the curving supportive strip that runs from the shoes' heels down toward the sole.*

D for Dassler and a logo that combined a word and an image. A common practice of cobblers of the time was to sew extra strips of fabric around certain sections of shoes to give those areas more support. Rudi invented a band of fabric called the formstrip that started at the heel and widened as it curved down to the sole, stabilizing the foot. Despite all the puma drawings Rudi made, the formstrip, doing double duty as a visual symbol and a stabilizer, became the official Puma logo in 1958. Ads showed a classic soccer shoe with the word *formstrip* written across the top.

As television gained steam as the most popular form of media, business owners began to see the importance of a logo as a tool for building a brand. Rudi had been years ahead of this trend when he named his company after an agile animal, but he hadn't yet created a logo that could embody the Puma brand. While the formstrip worked great on shoes, Puma was considering creating apparel. It wanted to create a tracksuit athletes could wear while warming up, but it first wanted to find a memorable and more modern logo.

Nuremberg cartoonist Lutz Backes was a friend of Rudi's son Gerd Dassler. At Gerd's request, in 1967 Backes sketched the jumping cat still used today. In the sketch, a puma jumps up with its long tail extended upward in the opposite direction. This cartoon logo has changed over the years, with minor details and the color altered, but Puma's modern logo still follows the spirit of Backes's original design. One of the most well-known iterations of the Puma logo features Backes's design of a puma jumping over the word *Puma*.

Once Rudi had a logo, he hired designers to start producing Puma tracksuits and sold them to teams.

PUMA INVENTS AND REINVENTS THE ATOM

When Rudi and Adi divided their company, they also split the employees. Rudi and the 14 Dassler Brothers Shoe Factory employees who followed him got to work right away.[2] From the start, Puma took the role of underdog against Adidas. While Adi had been sealing deals and operating the factory, Rudi had been at war. When Rudi started his company, he left

MILLION-DOLLAR PUMA

In perhaps one of the greatest lessons in the power of licensing, artist Lutz Backes was offered a choice of payment for his 1967 drawing of the Puma logo. The company would pay him either 600 German marks or the equivalent of about a cent for every item with the Puma logo that the company sold. Backes accepted 600 marks, which equates to a few thousand modern US dollars.[3] Puma also gave him shoes and a sports bag for his great artistic work. Had he accepted the other option, he would have become a multimillionaire.

behind all of the manufacturing machinery. Rudi and the Puma team were truly starting over from scratch.

Rudi kept up his commitment to specialization by meeting with athletes and coaches, asking about their firsthand experiences on the field, and incorporating their feedback into future iterations. In the world of product design, this process is known as user-centered design. In user-centered design, designers consider users and their needs when creating and revising. They also consult with users multiple times, giving them an active role in the design process. User-centered design gives the people who use the products more power in how they are made. Rudi then embraced the athletes' wins as Puma's wins as well. Rudi went about advertising just as he had previously—by partnering with talented athletes who had marketing appeal.

FIRST JOB AT PUMA

Georg Hetzler was one of the 14 employees who left the Dassler Brothers Shoe Factory and followed Rudi to Puma. Rudi hired 14-year-old Hetzler as an apprentice cutter in 1947. At that time, many young people took jobs as apprentices, learning a trade from someone who already did the job professionally. Hetzler decided to follow the man who hired him "even if that meant starting all over again."[4] Though he was only a young teen at the start of Puma, Hetzler's inside view of one of the biggest breakups in sports history has forever connected him to the Dassler family saga.

Rudi convinced some of West Germany's national soccer team players to wear Puma's first soccer shoe, the Atom, in the country's first postwar game against Switzerland. West Germany won the game, and Puma had its first hit with the Atom. Working with West German coach Sepp Herberger and other experts, Puma next developed the Super Atom, the first soccer shoe with screw-in studs. The invention was an upgrade for soccer shoes and established Puma as a lead innovator in sports gear. In late 1951, shortly before full-scale production of the Super Atom began, the Puma staff gifted Rudi a customized pair of golden Super Atoms. Puma often cites the Super Atom as a turning point for the company and its soccer heritage.

METAL STUDS

Before athletes could buy cleats, they gave their shoes more traction by hammering metal studs through the soles. The Dassler Brothers Shoe Factory was the first company to manufacture shoes with replaceable studs so they could be changed according to playing conditions. Puma was the first to make the studs out of nylon rather than metal, a change that made the shoes safer for players. The Super Atom took the innovation one step further with screw-in studs.

Next, Rudi and his team developed the Puma Brasil and outfitted German soccer team Hannover 96. In their Puma Brasils, underdogs Hannover 96 beat the favored club FC Kaiserslautern in the final match in Hamburg, and

> *Hannover 96, the 1954 German soccer championship winning team, wore Puma shoes in their victory.*

Puma launched an entire marketing campaign around the upset victory. Ads showed the German slogan "So war es in Hamburg," meaning "The way it was in Hamburg," along with photographs of the defining game moments, an illustration of the Puma Brasil, and a Puma logo.[5] The photos showcased the athletes' shoes. In a time before the modern sports media landscape, the marketing value of such images was priceless.

Rudi didn't stop with soccer shoes. Puma also created
shoes for runners. Puma's Oslo City debuted at the 1952
Winter Olympics in Norway. The style is named after the
capital city of the country and featured the words "Oslo
City" next to the Olympic five-ring logo on the side.[6]
In the 1960s, Puma released the Puma Suede, a break
from the usual sneaker material of regular leather. Puma
always strove to be the first to make new developments

Puma began with soccer, but the company expanded into a wide variety of other sports and activities. In the 1960s and 1970s, Puma offered shoes for wrestlers, parachutists, and boxers, among others. The company produced ice skates, roller skates, surf shoes, and bowling shoes. Rudi extended his practice of talking to professional athletes about their experiences to every sport he approached. Today, Puma focuses on fewer sports so it can invest more heavily in each category.

in footwear. Puma was the first company to use the vulcanization process to chemically bond the sole of the shoe to the upper part. Puma produced the first running shoe that featured Velcro. With each new silhouette, Puma took a step forward, laying the groundwork for a lasting business model.

PUMA BECOMES A SYMBOL OF PEAK PERFORMANCE

With every iteration and improvement, Puma continued to add to its reputation for a serious commitment to the pursuit of athletic excellence. When athletes stood out on the field, spectators could see which shoes were on their feet. The company saw particular potential in up-and-coming soccer players. Since Puma's largest market was soccer, a big name could bring Puma a lot of marketing power. Puma representatives approached athletes in locker rooms and at competitions, often through common friends, and worked to convince them

THE KING

B efore the Puma King, soccer shoes had solid, stiff soles that didn't allow for much movement. When soccer star Eusébio asked Puma to make him shoes that were more flexible, his request led to one of the most iconic cleats in soccer history. In his new superflexible Pumas, Eusébio was the top scorer at the 1966 World Cup. Puma honored Eusébio's accomplishment with the 1968 Puma King Eusébio, but the evolution of the King never stopped.

Puma continued to design lighter, softer, and more comfortable Kings. In 1970, Rudi Dassler's sons, Armin and Gerd, presented Brazilian soccer star Pelé with his own Kings before a World Cup tournament. Pelé wore the Kings when he led the Brazilian team to its third World Cup title and was named Player of the Tournament.

Many of the greatest players in soccer history wore Puma Kings. Argentina's Diego Maradona wore Kings when he scored what became known as the Goal of the Century in 1986. Lothar Matthäus of West Germany, who also wore Puma Kings, was named the FIFA World Player of the Year in 1991. The King still reigns. Brazil's Neymar Jr., one of today's best players, wears the most lightweight Kings to date, the King Platinum, and even helped to design a Neymar Jr. edition.

to wear Puma shoes. That process began to pay off during the 1960s and 1970s as the company built a reputation for extraordinary athletic achievement with Puma shoes.

In 1966, Portuguese forward Eusébio da Silva Ferreira, who was nicknamed O Rei, or the King, already wore Puma Wembleys to play when he requested shoes from Puma with a more flexible sole. Wearing these new shoes, Eusébio scored nine goals, becoming the top scorer in the 1966 World Cup. Puma next released the Puma King Eusébio in 1968, a silhouette that would remain a popular classic for many years to come and establish Puma as a symbol of ultimate athletic excellence in soccer.

Even today, few soccer players are as well known as Brazilian legend and Puma athlete Pelé, a man who many consider the greatest soccer player of all time. Pelé is the only player in history to win three World Cups and was named "Football Player of the Century" at the end of his career. In 1971, Puma designed the Puma Pelé Brazil to celebrate his accomplishments. The shoe featured Pelé's signature in gold foil lettering over a classic Puma design in Brazil's team colors of green and yellow.

Eusébio in his Puma shoes in 1969

CHAPTER FOUR

SNEAKER WARS

In some ways, the rivalry between the Dassler brothers served them both very well. Their drive to outperform each other motivated Rudi and Adi to lead their companies to achieve great levels of success. One way the competition played out was through the brothers' attempts to convince athletes to partner with their respective brands. In an era before athlete endorsements were common, Puma and Adidas compensated athletes— sometimes in gear, sometimes in cash—to wear their products. An athlete endorsement is a marketing strategy in which a business pays an athlete to spread awareness of the brand to their fanbase. No sporting event is more popular around the world

> *The fierce competition between Adidas and Puma has played out in sporting events, shopping malls, and marketing efforts for many decades.*

> *At the 1972 Olympics, officials made US sprinter and Puma endorser John Carlos put tape over the word* Puma *on his shirt.*

than the Olympic Games. That makes the Olympics a prime marketing opportunity. However, for many years the Olympics were limited to amateur athletes, or those who did not earn payment. Puma and Adidas took advantage of a gray area in the rules when they began to compensate Olympic athletes. Although not technically allowed, endorsements were an open secret.

The International Olympic Committee could have fought them more, but the birth of television played an important role in why it didn't.

Adidas and Puma already valued Olympic athletes for their ability to show how well the shoes performed in newspapers. Now that the games were being broadcast on television internationally, the marketing value of those athletes grew in leaps and bounds. Viewers became fans of specific athletes, and viewership of the Olympics rose when those athletes appeared. The Olympics had an interest in bringing in sponsors, and increased viewership was very appealing to advertisers. Athletes, corporations, and even the International Olympic Committee had a stake in allowing Olympic athletes to be sponsored by big business. Many sports historians suggest that the competition between Adidas and Puma to sign

WHEN ONLY PUMA WILL DO

In 1974, Puma-endorsed Dutch soccer player Johan Cruyff faced a big decision. The Dutch national team signed a deal with Adidas. That meant he would have to wear a jersey with that company's iconic three stripes. Cruyff famously argued that while his team may own his jersey, "the head sticking out of it is mine."[1] Ultimately, the team allowed Cruyff to wear a neutral uniform with no brand logo. In Puma's narrative, Cruyff refused to wear Adidas because of his love for Puma. When Cruyff won the Ballon d'Or, an award for the top male soccer player in Europe, for a third time, Puma built a marketing campaign around an image of the player in his one-of-a-kind jersey and Puma King boots with the caption "Johan Cruyff, European Superstar. Footballer of the Year with Puma."[2]

popular athletes sparked the widespread endorsement culture in pro sports today.

One of the athletes both companies pursued early on was German sprinter Armin Hary. Puma paid Hary to wear its sneakers during the final 100-meter race at the 1960 Summer Olympics in Rome. Hary wore Adidas for most of the day. But in his Pumas, Hary not only won his race but also broke a world record, becoming the first person to run the 100-meter dash in ten seconds flat. However, before Hary stepped onto the winners' podium to accept his medal, he slipped on his Adidas shoes, hoping to cash in from both Puma and Adidas. Instead, he enraged both companies. Adidas never worked with Hary again, and although Puma eventually forgave him and brought Hary on as a partner for a while, managers often referred to him as "a chap who eats on both sides."[3]

More athletes began to play the companies against each other to get better deals. Adidas and Puma, the biggest shoe manufacturers in the world, spent a lot of money trying to out-advertise each other. As a result, the companies made a deal they called the "Pelé Pact" in 1970. At the time, Pelé was the most popular soccer player in the world and was about to lead Brazil's national team to another World Cup win. Hiring him to endorse sneakers

> *Sprinter Armin Hary changed into Adidas shoes before the medal-awarding ceremony, upsetting Puma.*

would be incredibly expensive for either company, so Adidas and Puma agreed neither would make a deal with Pelé.

Just before the final match of the 1970 World Cup began, Pelé asked the referees for a moment to tie his shoes. After they agreed, Pelé bent down on one knee and the cameras panned down to broadcast the most popular athlete in the world tying the laces of his Puma sneakers. Unsurprisingly, the marketing teams at Adidas were livid to learn that Puma had reneged on the deal and paid Pelé to wear Puma shoes. Deals like this helped the rivalry between the companies earn the moniker "the sneaker wars." The Dassler brothers' feud and the resulting competition between Adidas and Puma endured through multiple generations. Many experts credit the rivalry for transforming sports apparel into the multibillion-dollar industry that exists today.

BROKEN PROMISES

Puma broke the Pelé Pact at the 1970 World Cup because after making the deal with Adidas, the company stumbled upon an opportunity that was too good to pass up. A company representative had been approaching other players to offer endorsements when Pelé asked why they weren't making offers to him, the biggest star of all. Without consulting anyone at Puma, the representative offered Pelé $120,000 to pull the shoe-tying stunt.[4] When the executives at Puma found out they had a potential deal with Pelé, they decided to renege on their deal with Adidas. The strategic move is often cited as a shrewd business decision.

THE BRUSH SPIKE BATTLE

Puma always kept its eye on improvement and wooed athletes with promises of enhanced performance. One of the ways Puma demonstrated good engineering was through the speed of the runners wearing its shoes. Competitors couldn't argue with broken speed records. In 1968, Puma created a limited run of the brush shoe, a running sneaker with a line of 68 tiny steel teeth under the ball of each foot.[5] Usually, running shoes had a smaller number of large spikes. The teeth, called spikelettes, were designed to better grab the new state-of-the-art, all-weather synthetic track that would debut at that year's Summer Olympics. The track was made from a brand-new type of running surface called Tartan, and the brush spikes were specifically engineered for running on it.

Puma kept the shoe design a secret until a few weeks before the 1968 Mexico City Olympics, when US Olympic officials built a practice track in a remote area for their athletes. The track was made of the new Tartan material so runners could get a feel for competing on it in a location where the weather conditions were like those in Mexico City. Puma representatives took their new running shoe to the athletes training there. In the few weeks when runners were allowed to wear the brush shoe, runners blew past world speed records. John Carlos ran the first under-20-second 200 meters ever recorded.[6] Vince Matthews broke a world record in the 400-meter dash, and Lee Evans then broke Matthews's record. As long-standing speed records fell, Puma's new brush shoe seemed impossible to beat. With only a few hundred pairs

> *The authorities banned Puma's new brush shoes from use in the 1968 Olympics.*

produced and the 1968 Summer Olympics weeks away, other runners caught wind of what was going on, and they all wanted the brush shoes.

In an unexpected turn, the sport's governing body announced that the brush shoes could not be worn in competition because they were too dangerous, and it overturned all of the records broken using the Puma brush shoes in the preceding weeks. Though no one can say exactly what motivated the governing body to make the decision, many rumors persist. The most common belief is that Adi Dassler's son, Horst, who was managing Adidas at the time, bribed the officials to deem the brush shoe illegal after witnessing its potential.

THE PURSUIT OF ATHLETIC EXCELLENCE

Puma managed to strike deals with some of the most popular athletes of all time. Puma had a proven approach. The company would meet with important coaches and athletes, find out their needs, and create products that made extraordinary athletes even better. It would celebrate athletes' wins and create marketing plans around game-changing moments. By emphasizing the connection between incredible sports moments and Puma, the brand's advertising appealed to athletes who pursued excellence. Puma engineered shoes to solve the problems inherent in any given sport, and it sought out athletes who not only were incredibly talented but also had star appeal. The result was an A-list roster of Puma ambassadors. Puma has teamed up with some of the most influential athletes in the world to help them break records and make their marks.

In 1954, German runner Heinz Fütterer broke the 100-meter world record in Yokohama, Japan, wearing Puma Makanudo running shoes, making him the fastest man in the world and athlete of the year. Four years later,

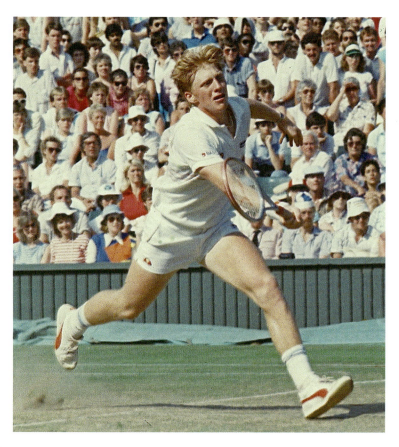

> *Boris Becker represented Puma during his historic Wimbledon victory in 1985.*

he broke the world record in the 4x100-meter relay in Pumas.[7]

Puma signed German tennis player Boris Becker as a brand ambassador in 1985 when he was still an unknown. At 17 years old, Becker was playing in custom red and white Puma sneakers and using a matching Puma racket when he became the youngest man to win Wimbledon. The tennis court at Puma headquarters in Herzogenaurach is named after the tennis legend, who went on to win six Grand Slam singles titles.[8]

From 1984 to 1987, Puma partnered with Martina Navratilova, a tennis phenom who won Wimbledon nine times and was named the Women's Tennis Association Athlete of the Year seven times.[9] As one of the first openly gay professional female athletes in the 1980s, Navratilova made a splash not only by being extremely talented but also by being outspoken and opinionated.

In 1997, Puma saw the potential in another young tennis player, Serena Williams. A teenager at the time, she was the younger sister of rising star Venus Williams, a Reebok athlete. When Puma met with Serena, the company's designers reported being impressed by the teenager bringing sketches of what she envisioned for herself. Even at a young age, Serena was a force who knew what she wanted. Serena eventually left Puma for a lucrative deal

FROM COURT TO RUNWAY

Serena Williams had impressive talent on the court from the start, but she also had a knack for envisioning standout fashion. With Puma, Williams developed some of her most show-stopping looks. Williams went against the tennis trend of skirts and starched white shirts in 2002 when she debuted her first catsuit at the US Open. The uniform was a form-fitting faux-leather one-piece made to move. The catsuit became a signature look for Williams.

PARTNERS FOR LIFE

Puma and Usain Bolt almost ended their partnership after a disappointing performance by Bolt in the 2004 Summer Olympics in Athens, Greece. But the sports brand has a reputation for loyalty, and so does Bolt, who never left Puma. Bolt's longtime manager announced in 2021 that Bolt and Puma had signed a unique lifetime partnership deal "not predicated on him being an athlete."[13] With Puma as a partner, Bolt is now a dancehall music producer with plans to branch out into different industries as a lifestyle athlete, a new type of entrepreneur who creates and markets products that appeal to the fan base they built while playing a sport.

with Nike, but Puma was her first major endorsement. In her autobiography, *On the Line*, Williams describes her feelings on receiving her first shipment of custom gear: "It was this moment, going through this giant box of Puma gear that all fit perfectly, where I felt I'd finally arrived as a player."[10]

Puma noticed sprinter Usain Bolt in 2002 when the 15-year-old began winning amateur track-and-field events that Puma sponsored in Jamaica. Between 2008 and 2009, Bolt broke the men's 100-meter world record three times. In 2009, at the Berlin Olympic Stadium—the same location where Jesse Owens wore Dassler Brothers shoes in 1936—Bolt smashed his own prior world record, running 100 meters in just 9.58 seconds.[11] Bolt, the fastest man alive, signed a lifetime contract with Puma, and in 2016 he thanked the brand that "stuck with [him]" from the beginning of his career.[12]

In its long tradition of finding athletes who stand out in the game and in their sense of style, Puma partnered with golf phenom Rickie Fowler when he turned professional in 2009. Known for wearing unusual patterns and bright, eye-catching colors like orange, Fowler and Puma brought a fresh young look to a sport known for its normally formal attire. Fowler and Puma have partnered with style visionaries to create limited lines of high-quality gear, shoes, and apparel.

CHAPTER FIVE

WINNING AND LOSING BASKETBALL

Puma targeted several sports with specially designed shoes. In the 1960s, the company turned its attention to a sport rising in popularity in the United States—basketball. Puma searched the horizon for basketball stars who had marketing appeal, and it found its man in Walt "Clyde" Frazier. Not only did the New York Knicks player perform on the court, but Frazier's flamboyant style also grabbed headlines. He wore fur coats and wide-brimmed hats like the one worn by Warren Beatty in the movie *Bonnie and Clyde,* which is how he got his nickname. Unsurprisingly, Frazier wasn't happy with standard-issue basketball sneakers. Puma approached him with its shoes, but

> Clyde Frazier became one of the athletes most closely linked with Puma in the company's history.

49

Frazier asked for some tweaks. He wanted a shoe that matched his singular style. Accustomed to the feedback process, Puma got to work engineering Frazier's vision. Aside from his technical requests, Frazier wanted Clydes of a different colorway for every game. Named after the player, the Puma Clyde was the first-ever signature shoe designed and named for a National Basketball Association (NBA) player.

WALT "CLYDE" FRAZIER

Walt "Clyde" Frazier worked with Puma to develop the company's first signature basketball sneaker. In Frazier's first contract with Puma, he specified what he wanted in a basketball shoe: suede instead of leather, "Clyde" printed on every shoe, and a new colorway for every game. Part of the deal was for Frazier to constantly send feedback to Puma so the shoes were always improving based on his experience.

Puma later released the Puma Ralph Sampson to honor the first pick in the 1983 NBA Draft. It became one of the most popular basketball silhouettes of the 1980s due to its lightweight construction and reputation for increased stability on the court. In typical Puma fashion, the company's designers met with basketball experts, listened to their feedback, and went to work. Sampson signed a deal worth hundreds of thousands of dollars, and Puma was poised for glory.

But a powerful rival would prevent it from taking the top spot in basketball shoes.

Puma's Sky LX was another popular shoe worn by NBA stars like Alex English through the 1980s. However, in addition to having to compete against the Sampson, it also went up against the enormously popular Nike Air Jordan. Performance-wise, some argued that the Puma Sky LX was superior to Nike's hit shoe. Sneaker expert Bobbito Garcia said, "The Jordan 1 paled in comparison to the Puma Sky LX, which was just a better ball-playing shoe."[1]

Puma's biggest misstep in basketball occurred in its partnership with Vince Carter, an up-and-coming player with a ton of potential whom Puma signed in 1998. Due to an NBA lockout, Carter's debut in Puma was delayed until 1999. The company was still working on designing Carter's signature shoe that shared his nickname, the Vinsanity, so he wore a pair of Puma Cell VIs in a series of ads. The Puma

THE PUMA DISC PROBLEM

Puma developed a laceless sneaker called the Puma Disc System Weapons in the 1990s. NBA player Cedric Ceballos wanted to play in the Sampsons he'd grown up wearing, but instead he was dubbed the "Discman" and became the face of the groundbreaking shoes. Excitement for the shoes grew after fans saw Ceballos in Puma Discs, but consumers couldn't find them anywhere to purchase because they weren't being sold in the United States. These glitches in communications and logistics signaled the beginning of the company's leanest years.

Cell VI exploded, becoming Puma's top-selling shoe ever, and much of the excitement came from the public believing the Cell VI was Carter's signature shoe. Carter appeared in several photos wearing the Cell VI, giving it tons of exposure. But once the Vinsanity was released, Carter played only two games in his first signature shoe before ending his contract with Puma and jumping ship for Nike. Most believe that Carter's main gripe with Puma was their delay in bringing his signature shoe to market.

Puma excelled at quality, but its competitors dominated in another key area: marketing. Especially in basketball, the signature shoe became the mark of success in the minds of athletes. Puma made a few

VINSANITY

Puma launched the Vinsanity with Vince Carter as part of a ten-year, $50-million deal during his rookie year.[2] The ad campaign featured a commercial that set the stage for Carter to take over the basketball world. The metal band Korn's song "Freak on a Leash" rumbles in the background while the camera cuts between a Puma-clad Carter showing off on a snow-covered street court and a professional court. The shot freezes as he dunks before flashing to an image of the shoe. Vinsanities never reached a wide public release before Carter ended his deal early. Slated to wear the Vinsanities at the 2000 NBA Slam Dunk Contest, Carter showed up in another brand instead.

> *Vince Carter worked closely with Puma, even participating in promotional photo shoots for the brand, but ultimately the partnership was short-lived.*

SNEAKERHEADS

In the late 1970s, hip-hop culture emerged. In addition to hip-hop music, it also involved fashion—including sneakers. People worked hard to find a signature style and often bought multiple pairs in case they wore out. As millions of identical Jordans flooded every mall, collectors developed a thirst for nabbing pairs from small runs of limited editions. Today the demand for these rare finds fuels an entire secondary market of sneaker resellers. The culture continues to thrive, with devoted fans of sneakers being known as sneakerheads.

more attempts to partner with NBA players, such as the 1980s Detroit Pistons player Isiah Thomas, but the relationships didn't last. Most of Puma's star NBA players wanted to play with the biggest company in the space, Nike. Puma attempted to keep its basketball division going for a time, but it eventually decided to exit the business, winding down its basketball shoe operations in the early 2000s. It would be several years before the company attempted a return to this major part of the athletic shoe business.

THE SUEDE

One long-lasting model for Puma has been the Puma Suede. In 1968, Puma released the Crack, a term that at the time meant something that was the best of its kind. Puma marketed the Crack as the shoe to wear with its first-ever apparel offering, the Puma tracksuit. When Walt Frazier asked for a shoe that could be produced in a multitude of colorways, Puma used the same suede material from the Crack because it was easy to dye. The Crack essentially became the Clyde.

Once Frazier's contract with the sneaker company ended in the 1970s, Puma could no longer use the name Clyde. Wanting to keep the popular style going, Puma renamed the silhouette the Suede. Hip-hop and break dancing culture adopted the Puma Suede as a style staple. The shoe became so closely associated with these US subcultures that Puma marketed them in the United Kingdom as Puma States. When the popularity of street skateboarding shot up in the late 1980s, skaters liked the Puma Suede for its comfort, durability, and range of colors. Thanks in part to its adaptability, the shoe has been a top seller for more than 50 years.

CHAPTER SIX

PUMA STANDS OUT

E ven as Puma focused on excellence in sports, the company made sure athletes looked good while competing. Puma was attracted to athletes like Walt Frazier and Serena Williams. They not only excelled in their sports but also showed off a great sense of style.

The athletic sneaker industry went through a huge transformation in the 1970s and 1980s that coincided with the birth of hip-hop. Sneakers became more about style than athletic performance. People began to wear them as everyday shoes instead of only when playing sports. Puma's Clydes in particular became a symbol of cool on both streets and high-school courts. Young players dreamed of

> *Over time, Puma products have grown popular not just as athletic wear but also as fashionable streetwear.*

succeeding in the NBA and having their own shoes one day like Frazier and Ralph Sampson.

The 1980s and 1990s were a slow time for Puma. Rudi's son Armin had attempted to work at his father's business, but there were frequent fights between the father and son, who didn't see eye to eye. Rudi permitted Armin to operate a factory called Puma Austria, but it was only a small subsidiary of Puma. However, as Rudi aged, he no longer had the stamina he once did. He asked Armin to return to the main company and began to relinquish more control to him, but the business stumbled as Nike and Adidas continued to dominate the sneaker fashion boom of the time. The hip-hop culture that brought sneakers to the forefront of everyday fashion also brought a ton of new competition in the form of brands like Reebok and Asics. Many talented employees fled Puma in the 1990s to work for its competitors. So did

EYE OF THE PUMA

One of the most striking visuals in Puma's marketing history comes from 1996, when British sprinter Linford Christie arrived at a press conference for the Olympic Games in Atlanta, Georgia, wearing blue contact lenses with a white Puma cat emblazoned on them. The move was especially bold because competitor Reebok had paid millions of dollars for exclusive advertising rights for the entire event. The oft-cited marketing stunt is a great illustration of Puma's outside-of-the-box approach to drawing attention to its athletes and, through them, its brand.

players and athletes. Puma may have made the first signature shoe for a basketball player, but Nike completely overshadowed it with the Air Jordan.

From the start, Rudi Dassler's company represented the underdog who steps up, performs its best, and upsets the favored team. The endorsement culture that Puma helped to create was now pricing the company out of the market. Puma would sign amazing athletes like Serena Williams and work with them up to the point when they were about to become superstars. Then the athletes would leave Puma behind for more lucrative contracts with the bigger companies. The company had to innovate to survive.

BACK TO THE DRAWING BOARD

Many long-running businesses are challenged as customers' needs change over time. Businesses need to adapt to cultural shifts. Otherwise, they lose their customers. Rudi and his son Armin, who was now leading the family business, had to change to stay competitive. Large shoe companies could mass-produce designer shoes cheaply, so Puma turned back to its original strength—specialization. Armin slimmed down the number of sports that Puma designed shoes for. The team could focus on making smaller batches of highly specialized shoes that filled a niche for people who

> *New CEO Jochen Zeitz took over Puma at a time when the brand was struggling.*

wanted optimized performance for their individual needs, not to mention standout style.

Through research and observation of trends, Puma had the foresight to know what its customers needed before they did. An example is the Fast Rider of the 1980s. Noticing a new emerging trend in recreational running, Puma designed a shoe for jogging. Unlike the running shoes that came before it, the Fast Rider was made for running on pavement instead of rubber tracks and designed in bright colors so runners could be seen in the dark. Throughout its history, Puma has found new ways to blend form and function.

In 1993, Puma appointed 30-year-old Jochen Zeitz as chief executive officer (CEO), making him the youngest CEO in German history to head a private company. Zeitz seized the opportunity to restructure Puma and revive its slumping sales through outside-of-the-box products. As an early adopter of the idea of corporate social responsibility, Zeitz also set out to redefine Puma's company culture through PumaVision, a commitment to recognizing the social and environmental responsibilities of corporations.

PIVOT TO FASHION

In 1998, Puma collaborated with Jil Sander, a German fashion designer with international name recognition and a minimalist aesthetic. These kinds of partnerships between shoe manufacturers and designers are common today, but the collection was out of the ordinary in 1998. The Puma x Jil Sander collaboration was the very first between a sports brand

and a fashion house. The line combined aspects of different shoes, such as the Fast Rider and the Roma, with colors and design elements inspired by Sander. It also included lifestyle versions of the King and Easy Rider. A lifestyle shoe is an everyday shoe that is inspired by a shoe that was designed specifically for a sport. The sports-inspired shoes that blended classic Puma silhouettes with modern style trends sold out immediately, and the sportswear and fashion collaboration was born.

Once Puma made this stunning turn in the direction of fashion in the late 1990s, the company doubled down on its success by collaborating with other style icons and brands that pushed the boundaries of shoes as fashion. In 2008, Puma hired Hussein Chalayan, a clothes designer known for thought-provoking fashions, as creative director. Next, Puma turned to the top pop and hip-hop stars for partnerships. Puma formed design

CALIFORNIA GIRLS

Puma developed the Cali in the 1980s. It was named after the California technique, a method of making shoes that women developed during the American Civil War (1861–1865). While most of the men were away at war, women back home came up with a way to produce shoes without using heavy machinery. Puma used an updated version of the method to create this classic silhouette, which is still being reissued today but now with eclectic designers and brands like Masaba Gupta, Selena Gomez, and L.O.L. Surprise freshening up the look.

> *Puma's racing boat,* Il Mostro, *sails into Boston Harbor in 2009.*

partnerships with stars like Solange Knowles, Kylie Jenner, and Young Thug. The company also experimented with moves into different sports. Puma entered its own sailing yacht, the *Il Mostro*, into the Volvo Ocean Race, one of the most challenging sailing races in the world. Puma partnered with several motorsports brands, including Mercedes, Ferrari, and BMW. It has also continued to provide performance racewear to F1 racers as well as lifestyle apparel for the racing fans in the stands.

In 2014, pop star Rihanna left her contract with Adidas to become creative director of Puma's women's line. Rihanna's Fenty x Puma line became a super popular trend after the Creeper design from her debut collection was named *Footwear News*'s Shoe of the Year in 2016. Since then, Puma has collaborated with a number of other well-known stars and brands to create shoes with an old-school feel and a completely modern style. Brands like Animal Crossing, Hello Kitty, and Sonic the Hedgehog, as well as fashion designer Alexander McQueen, have all become involved in Puma's shoes and apparel. Puma now hires athletic ambassadors and musicians like Selena Gomez and Dua Lipa, artists like Alexander-John, and social media influencers like Dixie D'Amelio to codesign and endorse its products. With each collaboration, brand-new markets and fans are created for Puma. The move to produce more collaborative products by interweaving the aesthetics of two very different brands started in footwear but was about to spread throughout the world of fashion. Collaborations became popular across several industries, and that trend still hasn't lost momentum.

With the rise of collaborations between fashion influencers and sportswear producers, another

> *Singer Rihanna is among the entertainment superstars who have been recruited by Puma.*

clothing trend began to take effect. Fashion used to be synonymous with dressing up, but the early 2000s saw huge growth in athleisure, a new category of clothing and footwear appropriate for both playing sports and everyday wear. The youth who adopted Puma Clydes as a fashion statement opened the door for sneakers and tracksuits to travel to the runway. Still today, Puma's designers see the company as a leader in athleisure design. Daniel Taylor, lead designer of sportstyle footwear at Puma, explains: "I think the reach and voice you can have as a creative within the company is unique to Puma."[1]

CHAPTER SEVEN

1952

SEVENTY YEARS LATER

Despite the relatively lean times for Puma in the 1990s, there were enough Puma fans to keep the brand going. Eventually the company managed to stage a comeback. In 2017, Puma broke its own sales records, earning more than four billion euros and showing growth in all divisions across the globe.[1] Puma proved that despite its struggles to adapt to a changing world, a success story remained possible.

The company couldn't have reached the 70-year milestone without the athletes and individuals who made Puma famous.

By 2018, the Puma brand had much to brag about after seven decades in the business of supporting some of the world's best athletes.

> *Longtime employee Helmut Fischer has curated a massive collection of Puma products celebrating the company's rich history.*

With a reputation for remembering the company's roots, Puma honored its founder with the Rudolf Dassler Legacy Collection in 2020. The collection featured a rerelease of the 1990s model of the Mirage, a silhouette that debuted as a track-and-field shoe with spikes in 1976. In the 1990s, Puma reimagined the classic and marketed it as a jogging and leisure shoe. The Mirage OG added updated technology to the original's structure and featured a metal charm in the shape of Rudi Dassler's original Puma logo design.

To celebrate, Puma hosted an exhibition of sports memorabilia from milestone moments in the brand's history at the company headquarters in Herzogenaurach. To mark the occasion, Puma constructed a pedestrian bridge that connects the original Puma offices with the new office space built to accommodate the company's forecasted growth. The bridge symbolically suggests Puma's dedication to innovating without forgetting the lessons learned along the way.

MR. PUMA AND THE ARCHIVE

For its seventieth anniversary, Puma designed a visual celebration of its most historic sports moments. Most of the exhibits would not have been possible without the contributions of a long-term Puma employee named Helmut Fischer. He has come to be known as Mr. Puma.

Fischer grew up next door to Rudi's son Armin Dassler in Herzogenaurach. He later played soccer for

Puma-sponsored FC Herzogenaurach before studying advertising. Armin hired Fischer as Puma's first marketing manager, and he handled everything from catalogs to media to running the tables at trade shows. He also worked one-on-one with many of Puma's biggest athletes to craft their promotional campaigns and signature products. Photographs of athletes posing with Fischer are a common sight in the halls of Puma's headquarters. Fischer said of his tenure, "I never doubted the strength of Puma, and so I stuck with our brand. Still today as almost 40 years ago—and with all my heart."[2]

THE WORLD'S FIRST SMART SHOE

Long before people had computers on their wrists counting every step they took, Puma recognized the importance of data to athletes. Puma worked with doctors to create the world's first smart shoe in 1985. The Running System Collection incorporated a tiny computer into the heel so runners could track their stats to learn more about their performance. This technology required runners to use a cable to transmit data from the shoe to a personal computer.

When Puma hired Fischer in 1978 to create a marketing department, the new employee stumbled upon an unkempt pile of old Puma designs in a small, dark room. Fischer, a lifelong collector of sports memorabilia, asked if he could be in charge of organizing and maintaining the collection. Fischer categorized every item in detail. As he

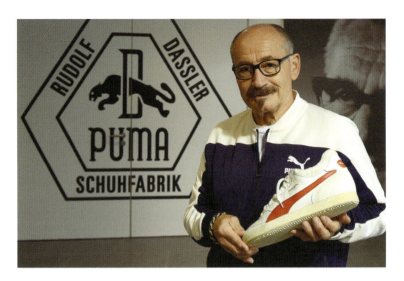

worked at Puma for decades, Fischer collected samples from every design stage of every shoe. When a Puma athlete won an event, Fischer saved not only the winning shoes but also newspaper clippings and photographs from the event.

In the 1980s, Puma suffered through major financial losses. Deutsche Bank seized control of Puma from the Dassler family heirs and ordered that any memorabilia related to the Dassler family be destroyed. Unable to fight the order, Fischer packed up all of the relics he had tirelessly assembled. He watched as they were hauled to the dumpsters. However, Fischer just couldn't sit by and watch his life's work disappear. Each night, he drove to the dumpsters to retrieve the boxes of prized Puma artifacts, take them home, and store them in his own garage. The collection grew so large that Fischer had to rent another garage with his own money to store his Puma collection. It wasn't until 2000 that he began to bring the items back to Puma headquarters.

Just before Puma's seventieth anniversary, professional archivists sorted and preserved the images, jerseys, and other memorabilia Fischer had collected since Puma hired him in 1978. Today, sports fans can visit the archives in Herzogenaurach to see some of the keepsakes on display. Images of athletes in historic sports moments sit next to the very Puma sneakers they wore in the photographs. Sometimes Puma takes parts of the exhibit on the road. None of it would exist if Fischer hadn't cared about Puma enough to rescue what he defines as "the existence and soul of Puma. These old things we build on."[3]

THE VALUE OF TRADITION

When former soccer pro Bjørn Gulden took the role of Puma's CEO in 2013, Fischer found someone else who saw value in his collection of nearly 8,000 shoes and hundreds of pieces of apparel, vintage advertisements, autographs, and anything else related to Puma.[4] In 2017, professional archivists renovated the area where the collection was stored so the items could continue to tell the story of Puma for many years to come. Puma also conducted interviews with many of the individuals involved so they could reflect on the details and aftermath of game-changing moments.

> *Puma's designers take inspiration from the past when developing new shoe models for the company.*

DIGITAL PUMA

Fischer's love of collecting every piece of the Puma brand resulted in something he couldn't possibly have foreseen when he began his collection. Professional archivists used three-dimensional (3D) scanners to scan all of the shoes Fischer collected. They created a digital database of every single shoe Puma ever made. These aren't just standard two-dimensional (2D) images but detailed 3D models. New generations of Puma creators now have access to every design idea conceived through the ages, and they can build on Puma's legacy. In the real world, nothing lasts forever, but at Puma, every design is now archived in computer memory. Designers no longer search Mr. Puma's cluttered shelves for an old Puma shoe. Now they need only search keywords in the database for images, dimensions, and the entire history of the product, including personal stories from athletes and Mr. Puma himself. Without realizing the significance of his actions, Fischer followed his sports collector's heart and inadvertently laid the groundwork for Puma's next wave of success.

The newest designers at Puma use the archive to mash up different styles. Designers can choose elements like fabric, lacing style, shape, or materials from different shoe iterations to create something entirely new. Many footwear designers come from backgrounds like industrial and automotive design and bring those style sensibilities to their designs of everyday shoes.

AUGMENTED REALITY (AR) SHOES

Puma dropped the LQD Cell Origin AR, the world's first augmented reality (AR) shoes, in 2019. The sneakers are covered In QR codes that can be scanned to unlock items in the Puma app. Depending on which part of the shoe is scanned, users can receive digital filters that apply different visual effects, such as making the shoes look as if they are on fire. Puma planned to add to the LQD Cell line, with each shoe offering new AR codes that unlock new experiences.

CHAPTER EIGHT

THE FUTURE OF PUMA

P uma celebrated 70 years of business success by not only looking back on its achievements but also looking forward to its vision of the future. Puma's "Forever Faster" mantra is a reminder that the company is still engaged in the pursuit of its number one goal: to be the fastest sports brand in the world by creating products that give even the best athletes improved performance. In 2018, Puma named the strategic priorities that would guide the direction of its future growth. They included innovation, distribution, trade, branding, women, basketball, local relevance, and sustainability.

For innovation, the company pledged never to stop challenging the status quo.

> *A large sign at a Puma office in France reminds workers and fans of the brand about a key part of the company's philosophy.*

77

In the areas of distribution and trade, it would work to make obtaining and distributing its products easier, faster, and more environmentally sound. For branding, the company would continue to make key athlete and influencer partnerships to strengthen the brand and keep it fresh. Puma would honor women as athletes and trendsetters by prioritizing the needs of female customers. One way Puma has made good on this promise is to increase the amount of research it does on female athletes and to provide better-fitting shoes specifically made for women. Puma also created She Moves Us, an online platform filled with stories of how female Puma athletes have overcome challenges.[1]

Puma would mount a strong comeback in the basketball shoe space. The company would increase the inclusion of athletes from every corner of the globe in its promotional materials so that young athletes all over the world have a chance to see their own local cultures reflected in Puma's brand. And finally, Puma would apply its renowned process of steady, incremental improvement to the goal of creating environmentally sustainable processes and products. This wide-ranging set of goals demonstrated Puma's intention to remain a powerful force in sports apparel and athleisure for another 70 years.

"INNOVATION IS NOT INVENTION"

The spirit of reinvention still exists at Puma from the top down. The sole focus of one group of employees is to help the entire Puma team approach their work with the same sense of constant improvement that Rudi Dassler brought to his company.

Restructured in 2021, Puma's innovation department guides all employees across the Puma brand to constantly challenge the status quo. The team still follows Rudi's original approach to design. Puma's senior head of innovation explains: "Innovation is not invention. Innovation is a process of constantly RE-inventing and evolving concepts based on expert research and user insights."[2] Puma maintains a close relationship with athletes not only for advertising but also for their help in Puma's eternal quest for better performance. The mission of the

ENVIRONMENTAL IMPACT

In 2011, Puma became the first major company in the world to assign an economic value to the environmental impact of its business. This new type of accounting measures not only profits but also Puma's Impact on people and the planet. Puma can identify which parts of its business cause the most environmental damage and prioritize tackling those issues head-on. Puma now has a sustainability department that keeps everyone across the Puma family focused on the goal of reducing environmental impact.

> *Puma's headquarters in Herzogenaurach is housed in an enormous complex. More than 1,000 people work there.*

innovation department is to "incubate experimental ideas and to inspire, through 'north star' projects."[3] Three main goals lead their research: helping athletes perform at their best, pushing the limits of footwear design, and working toward more sustainability in the company's products.

Puma realizes its commitment to innovation in several ways. The innovation team partners with universities to research human performance as it relates to biology and

technology. In the early days of Puma, individuals asked athletes and coaches about their personal experiences and explained what they learned to others. Through today's university partnerships, innovators use technology to digitally collect real-time data from thousands of college athletes as they practice and play. That data teaches Puma employees about athletes' needs much faster than one-on-one conversations. The innovation department has streamlined the system so that Puma is constantly gathering information for improvement.

FROM HERZOGENAURACH TO THE UNITED STATES

Herzogenaurach is still home to Puma's official headquarters, but the home base of Puma looks much different from its humble beginnings in the 1940s. Today the headquarters is a huge, glass-paneled building nestled among the houses of the picturesque Bavarian village.

Next door is a giant Puma outlet in a building designed to look like a Puma shoebox. A giant statue of the Puma logo leaps up in the distance. A full-size basketball court and soccer field with lights for night play sit in the middle of the Puma campus, ready for games at any time.

In 2021, Puma opened a new North American headquarters in Somerville, Massachusetts, complete with a roof deck, art

GOALS

In 2018, Puma beat offers by New Balance and Under Armour to partner with AC Milan, becoming the official global supplier and licensing partner with the 119-year-old Italian soccer club. Before the deal, AC Milan had partnered with Adidas for two decades. Both the soccer club and the apparel brand brought rich histories of athletic tradition to the partnership. From the beginning, Puma set out to make better shoes for soccer players, and it has continued with that mission across the globe.

installations, and a modern fitness center to attract top talent. The building features flexible office space so Puma can expand in the years ahead according to its long-term plans. Puma relies on the US market for a lot of its business. Most of the company's growth in the 2000s has been a result of its success in the North American and Latin American markets, so it's turning its attention to those consumers.

Puma kept its promise to expand in the US market with the 2019 grand opening of the Puma NYC flagship store, a sprawling 18,000-square-foot (1,670 sq m) showplace on Fifth Avenue in New York City that gives shoppers an immersive brand experience.[4] The interior is sleek and cool, with images of classic Puma sneakers, glossy photo displays of brand ambassadors from the sports and style worlds, and plenty of Instagram-worthy backdrops for

NBA 2K

The basketball section of Puma's NYC flagship store features stadium seating around a giant TV wall where customers can sit back and play a few rounds of the video game *NBA 2K*. Puma made a major return to the basketball space in 2018 with Roc Nation Sports CEO Jay-Z as creative director. Puma has begun appearing on the court with new sneaker designs, and the brand is popping up in unexpected places, including *NBA 2K*. Puma held a limited-time event called Puma Mania in which players could visit the virtual Puma store in the game, purchase Puma gear, and show it off during virtual play. Moves like this have shown that Puma remains as innovative in its marketing as it is in its shoe design.

visitors taking selfies, including a giant classic Puma Suede in red, large enough to fit a few people inside. The selection is a Puma-lover's dream with sneakers, apparel, and gear from every sport Puma covers. The Puma NYC flagship store is a monument to Puma's commitment to making a home in the US market and culture. Bjørn Gulden, CEO of Puma, says the store is part of Puma's goal to be "the fastest sports brand in the world" and a manifestation of Puma's commitment to pushing the boundaries of sports, fashion, and technology.[5]

Everything about the store falls in line with Puma's commitment to innovation through technology. That includes its immersive brand experiences and sports-engagement zones. Stores that serve more as a brand experience than a place to merely shop are becoming the next wave of large-scale advertising for future-focused businesses.

Puma is constantly coming up with creative ways for customers to customize their Puma merchandise so it best serves the users' needs and individual styles. Customers at the Puma NYC flagship store can personalize footwear, apparel, and accessories with style choices through high-tech options like 3D knitting and laser printing. One section of the store is dedicated to a space where artists can host demonstrations and events. For example, a demonstration from streetwear brand Chinatown Market allowed visitors to customize Puma gear using handheld printer guns.

SOCCER

I n its quest to design the ultimate soccer shoe through user-centered design, Puma has been studying the unique needs of soccer players since its early days. Soccer players interact with the ball mostly through their feet, so shoes are a pivotal piece of gear that can impact performance. Players need shoes that help them gain speed and traction, maneuver the ball, and stay comfortable simultaneously. Soccer shoes should fit snugly and feel like an extension of the player's body. They should be thin enough so the player can feel the soccer ball through the material of the shoe and as light as possible so players don't feel weighted down.

At the same time, they need to be thick enough to protect players' feet and equipped with spikes for stability. All of these factors help soccer players perform the quick, agile movements that score goals.

Puma often experiments with different fabrics to create new options. For instance, the coated mesh material of the Invicto Fresh allows heat to escape from the foot while keeping environmental moisture out, making for more comfortable play. The Ultra is made of a lightweight fabric called Matryxevo that is woven from Kevlar and carbon yarns and coated in a material called GripControl Pro, which improves touch and ball control. The Future Z 1.1 features an adaptive FuzionFit+ compression band that wraps around the midfoot for a "second-skin feeling." In agility tests, players achieved an average of 3 percent faster times in the Future Z than in its predecessor.[6]

CHAPTER NINE

FOREVER FORWARD

More than 70 years after Rudi founded Puma and more than 100 years since Adi cobbled shoes from scrap materials in their parents' laundry room, Puma is a multibillion-dollar corporation and one of the top three sneaker brands in the world.[1] Puma continues to break sales records by staying true to Rudi's original approach while also adopting new ideas. The company still partners with influential spokespeople and uses their input to design and improve new products, although these partnerships aren't only with athletes anymore. Though its connection to the soccer world is still deep, Puma has moved far beyond the soccer shoes it first started developing in the 1940s. Puma now

> *Shoppers around the world have helped Puma rebound from its struggles to become one of the top-selling sports apparel brands on the planet.*

partners with musicians, artists, fashion designers, and athletes involved in various sports around the world.

Over the years, Puma has survived family disputes, cutthroat competition, and a fickle market that nearly drove the shoe company to bankruptcy. However, Puma has also found countless ways to reinvent itself by partnering with icons outside of sports, becoming one of the main producers of athleisure apparel, collaborating with unexpected codesigners, and giving young employees the opportunity to set a bold course for Puma's future.

BACK TO THE OLD SCHOOL

Puma has committed to creating more products specifically for the North American market. For example, Puma reentered the basketball space in 2018. Creative director, former Brooklyn Nets owner, and CEO of Roc Nation Sports Jay-Z reimagined Puma's basketball division, reminding Puma of all the value in its history. "It's all about the Clyde," he advised Puma. "You gotta go back to the beginning to really reboot this thing."[2]

The result was the reimagined Clyde Court Disrupt, along with a roster of star NBA players signed as Puma ambassadors. Even original basketball partner Walt "Clyde" Frazier has come back to represent Puma as a lifetime brand ambassador. After two years as creative director, Jay-Z brought on Kyle Kuzma of the Los Angeles Lakers as a new face of Puma. Other Puma ballers include LaMelo Ball, Marcus Smart, Skylar Diggins-Smith, Breanna Stewart, Katie Lou Samuelson, and Jackie Young.

ONLY SEE GREAT

Puma's ad campaign Only See Great aims to spread positive energy through the life stories of its brand ambassadors. Puma has always partnered with icons who embody its values of strength, bravery, and endurance. The Only See Great campaign consists of interviews with sports icons in which they explore what it means to be great and describe the experiences and lessons that got them to where they are. Only See Great grew from an observation made by creative director Jay-Z: "I only see great. I don't see good. I don't see compromise. We should always strive to make something great, something that will last."[3]

EVOLUTION OF THE CLYDE

Codesigned with NBA player Walt "Clyde" Frazier, the original Clyde was the first flat basketball shoe. The Clyde gained popularity on both the court and the street. Break dancers, also known as B-boys, adopted them as a style staple in the 1980s, and the Beastie Boys rocked them in the 1990s. Much like Frazier himself, the shoe could excel on the court and make players look good doing it. Young players wore Clydes and thought about having their own shoes someday. However, as Puma lost its footing in the basketball space, Clydes fell out of fashion with players.

In 2018, the Clyde made a triumphant return led by Puma creative director Jay-Z, with a modern makeover that included the Clyde Court Disrupt. Puma ambassadors get to apply their own personal style details to the classic silhouette.

> *Soccer superstar Neymar Jr. has a major deal with Puma.*

BIGGER, BETTER DEALS

Despite the multitude of changes and new directions, Puma continues the soccer tradition that it forged with the Atom. Puma signed its largest soccer deal in history in 2019, officially partnering with Manchester City, Melbourne City, Girona, and Sichuan Jiuniu FC in a partnership that is the third most lucrative deal in the world of soccer. In a hint of what's to come, the CEO of Puma explained, "We want to maximize on-field performance as well as soccer culture, in areas such as music, gaming and fashion to connect and inspire the fanbase of each team."[4]

Puma, Nike, and Adidas remain the three biggest sports brands in professional soccer. In addition to soccer clubs, Puma also outfits several national soccer teams, including Italy, the Czech Republic, Morocco, and Ghana. Around the world, cricket, rugby, and handball teams play in Puma gear. Big names on the soccer field like Neymar Jr. and Kingsley Coman are exclusive Puma partners.

PEOPLE AND THE PLANET

In recent decades, Puma has prioritized being a positive force of change by focusing on sustainability. The company is a leading member of the Fashion Industry Charter for Climate Action, a group of businesses working with the United Nations to lower greenhouse gas emissions created by the fashion industry to net zero by 2050.[5] Puma uses its innovative approach not just in fashion and sports performance design but also in the design of production processes and the search for product materials. Puma has been conducting experiments on

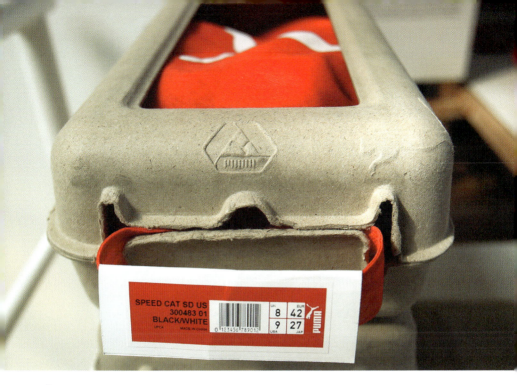

> *Developing new shoebox designs has been one part of Puma's overall sustainability efforts.*

processes aimed at reducing waste, including using more recycled materials in production, encouraging recycling through trade-in programs, and seeking out alternative environmentally friendly materials to replace the nonrenewable resources used in making sneakers. This level of commitment has resulted in some major advances, such as a biodegradable, suede-like textile. However, Puma seeks to revolutionize more than just its merchandise.

Puma set an ambitious goal to reduce the carbon footprint of its business offices by 35 percent and its entire supply chain by 60 percent by 2030.[6] Many of

Puma's offices are at least partially powered by renewable energy sources. The company committed to making radical changes like shifting to an even greater reliance on renewable energy sources and creating more products with ethically sourced raw materials. Puma promises to be a frontrunner in terms of responsible business leadership by expertly analyzing the way it does business and then making incremental changes to reach its sustainability goals.

The company website provides transparency by listing the suppliers Puma buys from and the facilities where its sneakers are made. Puma regularly audits shoe factories where its products are being produced to ensure that staff are being treated fairly in terms of pay, hours, and working conditions. These audits include private conversations with random members of staff. The company also created a worker complaint hotline for employees to bring problems to management's attention. Puma has zero tolerance for child or forced labor and will immediately cease business with a partner if these issues are discovered. The company is a member of the Fair Labor Association, a group of socially responsible organizations that advocate for greater accountability and transparency in how global businesses operate. On its website, Puma lists key sustainability goals, along with the status of its progress so far.[7]

REFORM

When Tommie Smith began running in college, white players were offered free shoes, but Black players were not. One day, a friend introduced Smith to Rudi Dassler, who started sending Smith Puma shoes and clothes. At the 1968 Mexico City Olympics, American sprinters Smith and John Carlos ascended the winners' podium and raised their fists in what many called a Black power salute. It was actually a sign of protest against apartheid, racism, and discrimination toward African Americans. Smith later explained that he meant his protest for all of humanity: "It was my stand for justice. . . . not for Black rights, it was for human rights."[8] Smith was largely ignored by the sports world

One way Puma supports its female athletes is by sharing the story of Puma athlete Sara Björk Gunnarsdóttir. Puma followed the Iceland national team captain from the beginning of her pregnancy, sharing her experiences via the She Moves Us platform. Puma continued following Gunnarsdóttir through motherhood and her return to the field. Puma planned to use the footage to produce a documentary about the struggles and benefits of balancing pregnancy, family, and a professional career in sports. Gunnarsdóttir offers her own insight and guidance to show that female athletes do not have to choose between having a family and a career in sports.

after the silent protest. His bravery essentially ended his sports career.

In 2018, Puma founded #Reform to honor the fiftieth anniversary of Smith's silent protest. Puma has made a commitment to partner with athletes and ambassadors "who have raised their voices to support universal equality."[9]

The objective of #Reform is to spread awareness about social issues such as problems in the US criminal justice system, the fight for LGBTQ+ rights, and gender equality. Puma supports the Black Lives Matter movement by donating to and promoting organizations that are working toward change. Puma partners with the Trevor Project to work toward more inclusivity for LGBTQ athletes. Puma has also worked on awareness campaigns with Football v Homophobia, the American Civil Liberties Union, and Women Win to promote change.

FORCES FOR SOCIAL CHANGE

One benefit of Puma's connection with so many amazing athletes around the world is the company's ability to bring together people who want to make the world a better place. These superstars have unique platforms from which to spread messages of social change. Puma encourages dialogue between people of different generations and cultures so they can learn from each other's experiences. In 2020, Puma brought together American sprinter Tommie Smith, British race car driver Lewis Hamilton, and French soccer coach Thierry Henry for a discussion on how race affected their experiences in the world of sports.

> *Tommie Smith,* second from right, *participated at an event for Puma's #Reform initiative in 2018.*

Puma reinvented itself for a modern world by investing in its athletes, celebrating their achievements, and perfecting the process of design by collaboration. Through decades of wins and losses, the people who stayed loyal to Puma made the company what it is today. With the goals of expansion, constant innovation, sustainability, and celebration of all the unique athletes it serves, Puma has proven its dedication to its mission of helping athletes be forever faster.

ESSENTIAL FACTS

KEY EVENTS

- Rudolf (Rudi) and Adolf (Adi) Dassler found the Dassler Brothers Shoe Factory in Herzogenaurach, Germany, after World War I.

- Jesse Owens wins four gold medals during the 1936 Berlin Olympics while wearing Dassler Brothers spikes.

- Rudi Dassler is drafted during World War II and deployed to the front lines.

- After 28 years in business, the Dassler Brothers Shoe Factory closes its doors in 1948, and a month later Rudi founds Puma.

- Puma breaks an agreement made with Adidas not to make a deal with soccer star Pelé when Pelé accepts money to wear Puma shoes during the 1970 World Cup.

- Puma celebrates its seventieth anniversary in 2018 with an exhibit of Helmut Fischer's archival collection and a return to basketball with Jay-Z as creative director.

- The Puma NYC flagship store opens on Fifth Avenue in 2019, providing a wide selection of Puma merchandise and an immersive way to experience the Puma brand.

KEY PEOPLE

- Rudi Dassler is the founder of Puma.

- Helmut Fischer becomes known as Mr. Puma because of his long tenure at the company and his vast collection of Puma memorabilia.

- Armin Dassler, Rudi's son, becomes CEO of Puma after his father retires.

- Former professional soccer player Bjørn Gulden becomes Puma's CEO in 2013.

KEY PRODUCTS

- Oslo City: Introduced at the 1952 Winter Olympic Games in Norway, the classic design serves as the base for multiple reboot designs.

- Puma Suede: The Puma Suede hit the streets in 1968, gaining popularity in both the sports world and hip-hop culture.

- Puma Clyde: The Clyde, created in collaboration with Walt "Clyde" Frazier, was the first-ever signature shoe named for a National Basketball Association (NBA) player.

- Mirage OG: A timeless silhouette that's gone through several redesigns, the Mirage OG first launched for track and field in the 1970s and later for jogging in the 1990s.

- Ultra 1.3: The lightest soccer shoe on the market, the Ultra combines research-driven technology and innovative design.

QUOTE

"Rudolf's vision was that all of his products would embody the characteristics of a Puma cat: speed, strength, suppleness, endurance, and agility—the same attributes that a successful athlete needs."

—Longtime Puma employee Helmut Fischer

GLOSSARY

ambassador
An individual authorized by an organization or company to represent it or its products.

apprentice
A position for a person learning a trade.

archive
An organized collection of historical items that is managed by a person or organization.

cobbler
A person who makes and fixes shoes.

colorway
A color or set of colors in which a product is available.

entrepreneur
A person who organizes and operates a business or businesses.

flagship store
A lead store that works as a showcase for a brand.

licensing
Paying for the right to use another person's design for a limited time.

mash-up
A new product that serves as a bridge between two or more ideas.

rivalry
A heated competition between two parties over a long period.

secondary market
A market in which people sell merchandise, such as sneakers, that they already own.

silhouette
The shape of a specific model of shoe.

simulator
A machine that replicates the experience of operating a vehicle.

specialization
The process of focusing one's efforts in a single area.

3D scanners
Devices used to create three-dimensional digital representations of real objects.

vulcanization
A method of chemically treating rubber or plastic to change its physical properties.

ADDITIONAL RESOURCES

SELECTED BIBLIOGRAPHY

CATch-up: Puma's Employee Magazine, n.d., puma-catchup.com. Accessed 4 Dec. 2021.

"Puma Archive." *Puma*, n.d., about.puma.com. Accessed 17 Jan. 2022.

Smit, Barbara. *Sneaker Wars: The Enemy Brothers Who Founded Adidas and Puma and the Family Feud That Forever Changed the Business of Sports.* HarperCollins, 2008.

FURTHER READINGS

Kortemeier, Todd. *AC Milan*. Abdo, 2018.

McKinney, Donna B. *Excelling in Soccer*. ReferencePoint Press, 2020.

Streissguth, Tom. *Adidas*. Abdo, 2023.

ONLINE RESOURCES

To learn more about Puma, please visit **abdobooklinks.com** or scan this QR code. These links are routinely monitored and updated to provide the most current information available.

MORE INFORMATION

For more information on this subject, contact or visit the following organizations:

PUMA HEADQUARTERS

Puma Way 1
91074 Herzogenaurach, Germany
+49-9132-81-0
info@puma.com

The Puma headquarters is located in Rudi Dassler's hometown, Herzogenaurach.

PUMA NORTH AMERICAN HEADQUARTERS

455 Grand Union Blvd.
Somerville, MA 02145
978-698-1000

Puma's North American headquarters is found in Somerville, Massachusetts.

PUMA NYC FLAGSHIP STORE

609 Fifth Ave.
New York, NY 10017
917-594-5161
https://us.puma.com/us/en/nyc
customerservice.us@puma.com

Puma's location on Fifth Avenue in New York City is the only Puma flagship store in the United States.

SOURCE NOTES

CHAPTER 1. FOREVER FASTER

1. "Puma Skill Cube Lets You Train with Your Favorite Sport Stars." *DesignWanted*, 2 Apr. 2020, designwanted.com. Accessed 18 Mar. 2022.

CHAPTER 2. BROTHERS DIVIDED

1. "'Our Strength Lies in Specialization.'" *CATch up*, 9 Nov. 2018, puma-catchup.com. Accessed 18 Mar. 2022.

2. "Puma Timeline." *Puma*, n.d., about.puma.com. Accessed 18 Mar. 2022.

3. "Jesse Owens." *Encyclopedia Britannica*, n.d., britannica.com. Accessed 18 Mar. 2022.

4. Kate Connolly. "Adidas v Puma: The Bitter Rivalry That Runs and Runs." *Guardian*, 18 Oct. 2009, theguardian.com. Accessed 18 Mar. 2022.

5. "The Fascinating Family Feud That Led to Adidas and Puma." *Today I Found Out*, 16 Oct. 2017, todayifoundout.com. Accessed 18 Mar. 2022.

6. Barbara Smit. *Sneaker Wars: The Enemy Brothers Who Founded Adidas and Puma and the Family Feud That Forever Changed the Business of Sports*. HarperCollins, 2008.

CHAPTER 3. BECOMING PUMA

1. "How the Jumping Cat Was Invented." *CATch up*, 15 Mar. 2016, puma-catchup.com. Accessed 18 Mar. 2022.

2. "Happy Birthday, Puma!" *CATch up*, 1 Oct. 2018, puma-catchup.com. Accessed 18 Mar. 2022.

3. "How the Jumping Cat Was Invented."

4. "Happy Birthday, Puma!"

5. "Puma Timeline." *Puma*, n.d., about.puma.com. Accessed 18 Mar. 2022.

6. "PUMA Oslo-City." *Frixshun*, n.d., frixshun.com. Accessed 18 Mar. 2022.

CHAPTER 4. SNEAKER WARS

1. Peter Kenny Jones. "Two Stripes: How Sponsorship Conflict Made Johann Cruyff Play the 1974 World Cup with a Two Striped Adidas Kit." *Footy Analyst*, 12 July 2020, footyanalyst.com. Accessed 18 Mar. 2022.

2. Jones, "Two Stripes."

3. Barbara Smit. *Sneaker Wars: The Enemy Brothers Who Founded Adidas and Puma and the Family Feud That Forever Changed the Business of Sports*. HarperCollins, 2008. 50.

4. Brian Cronin. "Was Pele Paid to Tie His Shoes during the 1970 World Cup Final?" *Los Angeles Times*, 15 Oct. 2012, latimes.com. Accessed 18 Mar. 2022.

5. "Annual Report 2018." *Puma*, 2018, annual-report.puma.com. Accessed 18 Mar. 2022.

6. Michael McKnight. "A Brush with Greatness: The Puma Shoe That Upended the 1968 Olympics." *Sports Illustrated*, 15 Nov. 2019, si.com. Accessed 18 Mar. 2022.

7. "Puma Timeline." *Puma*, n.d., about.puma.com. Accessed 18 Mar. 2022.

8. "On Center Court with Boris Becker." *CATch up*, 25 Aug. 2020, puma-catchup.com. Accessed 18 Mar. 2022.

9. "Puma Timeline."

10. Aaron Dodson. "The Little-Known Story of Serena Williams' First Endorsement Deal." *Andscape*, 24 Sept. 2021, andscape.com. Accessed 18 Mar. 2022.

11. Michael Benson. "Legendary Moment." *Talk Sport*, 1 Aug. 2021, talksport.com. Accessed 18 Mar. 2022.

12. Lucy Handley. "Puma Has Stuck with Me through Everything: Usain Bolt." *CNBC*, 29 Nov. 2016, cnbc.com. Accessed 18 Mar. 2022.

13. Donovan Watkis. "Usain Bolt Signs Lifetime Partnership Deal with Puma." *Dancehall Mag*, 17 June 2021, dancehallmag.com. Accessed 18 Mar. 2022.

CHAPTER 5. WINNING AND LOSING BASKETBALL

1. Aaron Dodson. "The Forgotten History of Puma Basketball." *Andscape*, 5 Feb. 2019, andscape.com. Accessed 18 Mar. 2022.

2. "Vince Carter's Puma Vinsanity Shoes." *What Pros Wear*, 27 Dec. 2019, whatproswear.com. Accessed 18 Mar. 2022.

CHAPTER 6. PUMA STANDS OUT

1. "Behind the Scenes of Creativity." *CATch up*, 28 June 2021, puma-catchup.com. Accessed 18 Mar. 2022.

SOURCE NOTES CONTINUED

CHAPTER 7. SEVENTY YEARS LATER

1. "Cracking the 4 Billion Euro Mark." *CATch up*, 12 Feb. 2018, puma-catchup.com. Accessed 18 Mar. 2022.

2. "An Interview with Helmut Fischer aka 'Mr Puma.'" *Frixshun*, n.d., frixshun.com. Accessed 18 Mar. 2022.

3. "Puma Archive: The Discovery." *YouTube*, uploaded by PUMA Group, 6 Dec. 2018. Accessed 18 Mar. 2022.

4. "Helmut Fischer, Puma." *Premium Group*, n.d., premium-group.com. Accessed 18 Mar. 2022.

CHAPTER 8. THE FUTURE OF PUMA

1. "She Moves Us." *Puma*, n.d., about.puma.com. Accessed 18 Mar. 2022.

2. "Challenging the Status Quo." *CATch up*, 30 Nov. 2021, puma-catchup.com. Accessed 18 Mar. 2022.

3. "Challenging the Status Quo."

4. Marc Bain. "At Puma's New Flagship, You Come to Shop but Stay for the F1 Racing Simulators." *Quartz*, 29 Aug. 2019, qz.com. Accessed 18 Mar. 2022.

5. Emily Engle. "A Look inside Puma's 18,000 Square Foot Fifth Avenue Flagship Store." *Hypebeast*, 28 Aug. 2019, hypebeast.com. Accessed 18 Mar. 2022.

6. "Neymar Jr and Puma Invite You into the World of Future Z." *Neymar Jr*, 10 Jan. 2021, neymarjr.com. Accessed 18 Mar. 2022.

CHAPTER 9. FOREVER FORWARD

1. Zak Maoui. "Best Puma Shoes to Buy Right Now." *GQ Magazine UK*, 28 Mar. 2021, gq-magazine.co.uk. Accessed 18 Mar. 2022.

2. Aaron Dodson. "The Forgotten History of Puma Basketball." *Andscape*, 5 Feb. 2019, andscape.com. Accessed 18 Mar. 2022.

3. "Usain Bolt Talks 'Only See Great.'" *CATch up*, 5 Jan. 2022, puma-catchup.com. Accessed 18 Mar. 2022.

4. "Puma Signs Record-Breaking $860 Million Partnership with Manchester City." *CNBC*, 12 Sept. 2019, cnbc.com. Accessed 18 Mar. 2022.

5. "About the Fashion Industry Charter for Climate Action." *United Nations Climate Change*, n.d., unfccc.int. Accessed 18 Mar. 2022.

6. "Climate Change." *Puma*, n.d., about.puma.com. Accessed 18 Mar. 2022.

7. "Staying on Target." *Puma*, n.d., about.puma.com. Accessed 18 Mar. 2022.

8. "Interview with Helmut Fischer about Track & Field Legend Tommie Smith." *CATch up*, 16 Oct. 2021, puma-catchup.com. Accessed 18 Mar. 2022.

9. "Reform." *Puma*, n.d., about.puma.com. Accessed 18 Mar. 2022.

INDEX

ABOUT THE AUTHOR

Marie Jaskulka grew up in Philadelphia, Pennsylvania, before moving to places like Ireland and Alaska and settling down in Swoyersville, Pennsylvania. When she's not writing, she's hanging with her daughter or dabbling in photography and yoga. Marie is the author of *The Lost Marble Notebook of Forgotten Girl & Random Boy* and a biography of rapper Tyler, the Creator.

ABOUT THE CONSULTANT

Kelly Cobb is an associate professor at the University of Delaware in the Department of Fashion and Apparel Studies, where she teaches and conducts research in the areas of sustainable design, fashion communication, and strategy. She lives in Philadelphia with her media expert partner and Lego expert daughter. She loves hiking, creating, and collaborating with students and the fashion industry. In this way, she contributes to what fashion can be: connective, reflective, expressive, and transformative.